Anonymous

The Life of Dick En-L D, Alias Captain En-L D

Or turf memory. With notes and illustrations

Anonymous

The Life of Dick En-L D, Alias Captain En-L D
Or turf memory. With notes and illustrations

ISBN/EAN: 9783337185169

Printed in Europe, USA, Canada, Australia, Japan

Cover: Foto ©Raphael Reischuk / pixelio.de

More available books at **www.hansebooks.com**

THE
LIFE

OF

DICK EN-L—D,

ALIAS

CAPTAIN EN-L—D;

OF TURF MEMORY.

WITH

NOTES AND ILLUSTRATIONS.

" I fhall a tale unfold, whofe lighteft words would harrow
" up the foul, freeze the young blood,"————-

SHAKSPEARE.

LONDON:

PRINTED FOR T. BOOSEY, NO. 4, OLD BROAD-
STREET, NEAR THE ROYAL-EXCHANGE;

AND TO BE HAD OF ALL THE BOOKSELLERS IN WEST-
MINSTER AND THROUGHOUT THE KINGDOM.

M DCC XCII.

[Entered at Stationers-hall.]

TO THE

P U B L I C,

AND MORE PARTICULARLY TO THE

TWO UNIVERSITIES OF

CAMBRIDGE and OXFORD;

S C H O O L S

O F

WINCHESTER, ETON, WESTMINSTER,

AND H A R R O W;

AND ALL THE

LEARNED ACADEMIES

THROUGHOUT THE KINGDOM,

THIS

W O R K

IS

HUMBLY AND MOST RESPECTFULLY

D E D I C A T E D.

PREFACE.

PERHAPS fome apology may be confidered requifite for this publication :—the Author's plea is, the good the work may do to millions, and no mortal injured. We declare we have no ambition to gratify; no refentment lurking in our hearts: nor is there an iota through the book, but what are well-known facts; though not univerfally known.

We flatter ourfelves that examples of fo dreadful a nature, will

be

be ferioufly confidered by thofe,
whofe youth pleads a powerful
reafon why they are not acquainted
with vices of fuch enormity; that
unlefs moft of the facts were not
upon record, or told and vouched
by the firft authority, gentlemen
who would fhrink from detraction,
as from a deadly fin; and men
whofe whole life have been a con-
catenation of all that can be confidered great and good; or this
work fhould not have made its
appearance.

Formerly it were confidered a
leading principle to refine the feel-
ings of the heart; to give by example, a love to moral excellence;

to

to invite and infpire by family-
pictures, a reverence for learning
and virtue; and to fhew the de-
formity of vice, and hold the
mirror up to nature. We wifh
we could fay the practice was in
its full vigour; at prefent we fee
our noble youths betting at a cock-
fight or horfe-race, as if the fal-
vation of their country depended
on the number of bets they made;
and what is worfe, rather than not
bet at all, fay done for fifty or
a hundred, to the very rafcal that,
perhaps, fix hours afterwards ftops
him, and bids him deliver, money—
or life. Indeed, the laft *bufinefs* is
by much the moft harmlefs; and

a   there

there are few, if any, good parents that would not rather have their son robbed on the highway of a few guineas, than pillaged of his estate or reversion, at a gaming-table.

If, therefore, this little work will awaken and guard the credulous from not playing at all; or, if they must play, play for trifles with men of honour; and put the winnings into a box for the benefit of the miserable ef every description: we may then cherish a hope that our rising generation may emulate the Greek and Roman name, when in their plenitude of glory, and enjoyment of all their liberty so

dearly

dearly purchafed. We are forry to conclude, that gaming brought on intemperance, and every fenfu- ality ; and ended at laft in a levity that loft them their moft invaluable bleffings; namely probity, courage, prudence, and empire.

THE

THE
BIOGRAPHER's LIFE.

THE Author means not to take up much of the reader's time; but by way of expiation to furnish the public with a life of the biographer. He was born in the county of H——, defcended from an illuftrious and honourable family, his father having ferved in three fucceffive parliaments, in the reign of George I. and II. and having but two fons, one he fent to Cambridge, and the author of this work to Winchefter; where having difcovered great natural powers, and from fuch a difcovery ought to have been tranfplanted, like a fine exotic, to a more exuberant foil, he was (unluckily for him) prefented with a pair of colours in the guards.

Nothing

Nothing particular happened from seventeen to twenty-two : gaming, drinking, wh——, and mounting guard about twice a month, were his only ftudies. Being what the females call a pretty fellow, they now and then invited him to their routs, card parties, &c. &c. till having entered into his twenty-fixth year, a lady whofe perfonal charms were not very attractive; but fhe had near eighty thoufand pounds in hard cafh, and a very amiable difpofition : a match foon took place, and the poffeffion of fo much money made our author believe that fuch an immenfe fum could never be fpent. He was very much efteemed, gave great dinners, fplendid routs, fine liveries, and an elegant eqiupage ; and for his own fake we wifh he had done no more. He entered into deep play, kept running horfes, did or appeared to do equal with any nobleman of fifty thoufand a year ; but he had forgot the moft important matters, namely that his various

expences

expences for running horfes, grooms, dice, cards, &c. would in about two years, as he always played with honour, fwallow up the fortune his worthy wife brought him, and his whole fund would be exhaufted. His brother, one of the moft amiable men on earth, gave him a friendly hint, that he thought he was going on too faft, " No," replied our biographer, " let me alone, I am myfelf confidered a deep one;" and fo far as great knowledge, infinite addrefs, a winning difpofition, he was confidered to amply poffefs : but pity it is that fuch attractive powers makes entirely againft a generous-hearted gamefter. In fhort, he was in five years eafed of the trouble of keeping a banker, and a long ftring of fine race-horfes, brood-mares, &c. were fent to the hammer, one after another, till all his ftables in town and country were cleared: the maffy fideboard, the fplendid laced liveries, were difpenfed with ; and the elegant houfe, with all its magnificent

furniture,

furniture, fent to Skinner's; and to a wor=
thier man ·they could not be fent.

He now began to pull in (a turf phrafe)
and when he gave himfelf time to examine his
own affairs, he found the account run thus:

Debtor.	Creditor.
Wife's fortune .. 80,000	To receiving a know-
Her health de-	ledge of the flang 00,000
clined.........	Ditto to drinking
To fix friends, bor-	hard......... 00,000
rowed of each	Ditto to out-living
2,000l 12,000	every friend on
To annuities grant-	earth but my
ed feven people	brother and ano-
for 100l. per an-	ther gentleman 00,000
num, at feven	Ditto to know how
years purchafe 4,900	to bleed a horfe
To a lofs of health,	Ditto to taking
friends, and a	fnuff with a pe-
great memory	culiar grace....
£ 96,900	£ 00,000

We will leave our readers to judge of
this laft acquifition, and, except bleeding a
horfe; for we hold it humane to know
aught that can do fo noble an animal good;
we fhall not be thought vain in pronouncing
the credit fide of NO USE.   .

T H E

THE

LIFE

OF

DICK EN-L—D,

ALIAS

CAPTAIN EN-L—D;

OF TURF MEMORY.

A S the anecdotes of this hero would alone fill a volume in folio, we muſt content ourſelves with guarding the riſing age of the learned ſeminaries; and happy, thrice happy ſhall we be, if they will totally avoid (by thoſe characters being ſhewn with rigid truth and impartiality) not only the turf, but every gaming-houſe where any of the black-leg tribe reſort.

B   Dick

Dick En–l—d is a native of Dublin; and had he been content with following the occupation of a fcene-fhifter, and not left his native foil, many a worthy, though credulous charaƈter, would now have enjoyed the comforts attendant on independance and a polifhed education. Nurfed in the lap of vice, and dead to all moral reƈtitude, he quitted the only honeft employment he ever had, to embrace (and *fhifted* to) every fcene of infamy. At laft, making too *free* with a gentleman in Dawfon-Street, he was purfued, taken, and fent to gaol; from which place he broke out and embarked for England. His firft effay was at a brothel at Charing-Crofs, in the charaƈter of porter; being very robuft, he got promoted to the *high honour* of bully : not content with his noƈturnal depredations on the druken failor, or feduced youth; he had at one period twenty-three wh—es *

that

---

* We blufh to inform our readers, that in a city like this, where a well regulated police fhould proteƈt thefe unhappy females, thoufands are nightly driven by diftrefs and bad ufage to obtain a miferable exiftence; and out

of

that paid tribute to him. Every feeling heart muſt ache, to think of the miſeries thoſe innocent and much to be pitied victims undergo. After about nineteen months, our hero quitted his employment to embrace that of marker at a billiard table— where finding a *jontleman* congenial to his own *purity* of mind, they put on fine clothes, and dreſt, or rather attempted to dreſs, like gentlemen ; but in that they foiled themſelves, and were ever the butt of ridicule. Indeed, the one looked like Tom Errand in Beau Clincher's clothes ; his colleague, who had juſt left off a poſtillion's jacket, looked and walked a very groom indeed.

We now ſee our fraters in vice, ſtrutting and looking big wherever they could thruſt their faces ; indeed, they wanted to be in

of every guinea the pander receives five ſhillings in the pound.

As the new police has already given excellent proofs of their intentions to reform, we feel infinite comfort in the hope, that the poor deluded forſaken females, once the delight of their fond parents, will be reſtored to ſociety.

good

good company, though neither of them could read writing; an *error*, no doubt, in their *preceptor:* no matter, what ever were their defects, the two captains (for they wore cockades) kept a good look-out at Bolton's for their countrymen, and laid them under heavy contributions.

A thoufand inflances is known to the world, though not fufficiently; among their various arts, they claimed a knowledge of *all* the firft families in Ireland ; and though very ftrange, yet true, a number of un-fufpecting real gentlemen believed their ftory.

The Chefter coaches bringing at leaft twenty Hibernians every week, it will be readily admitted they had a conftant fup-ply of dupes. While they had cafh, Dick catered for their various appetites, women, or ***, wine, or play, they would have as long as they had a guinea—but no lon-ger.

From an obfcure lodging we now find Dick in a neat houfe in St. Al—n's-Street; and the little groom, alias Capt. Wa—ce, in another in S——k-Street, in the treble

capacity

capacity of pimp, greek *, and bully; and having by threats frightened many timid fouls, at laft accumulated a fum fufficient to buy a lieutenancy in the army, and then our two *worthies* quitted partnerfhip.

It muft raife the admiration of every thinking mind, how two fuch mifcreants, without a particle of education, family-connexion, or addrefs, could ever get a real gentleman to affociate with them : the truth is, there is no fwallow like an Englifh-man's; and all they wanted was a fingle

---

* A greek is the prefent modern phrafe for a black-leg, who frequents horfe-races, cock-fights, and billiard-tables in the day time ; and that he may not be idle, for it is a regular vocation, they are at every gaming-table they can thruft themfelves into, from about eleven at night, to fix, feven, or eight in the morning, in the *upright* trade of cogging a die, or flipping a card, to the great terror of all worthy parents, and *certain* deftruction to the health, morals, and fortune of every young man in the kingdom ; from the fon of a duke, to the offspring of every refpectable citizen.

When they do take an early hour to reft, it is when there is not a fingle pigeon to be found. The lower order of greeks call pigeons Flats ; if we may be allowed a mufical fimile, we hope the flats will foon become *fharp* enough to keep themfelves in unifon.

hour

hour at dice, or any other game; they had reduced winning to a certainty, and the lofers had to choofe—pay, fight a duel, or be docked *. At the latter work Dick was expert; for inftance, playing one night with a Frenchman, T––t, a watch-maker,

* This polite operation was performed in a tavern at Charing-Crofs, the mafter of the houfe telling the ftory to all his company for weeks afterwards, and fpoke of it as a matter of prowefs in Dick—*for even Dick had his friends*—and every low greek exulted in. fo *magnanimous* a tranfaction; but poor G—y Ma—n, docking or caf-tration, as Dick called it (for Dick knew not the dif-ferent interpretation of the word) for poor G—y was punifhed on bare fufpicion; for having one evening called in St. Al—n's-Street to drink a cup of tea with Mrs. En–l—d, Dick unluckily interrupted them, and infifted upon his either fighting a duel, or by *Jafus* he would dock him: in vain did they affert their innocence, in vain did they fupplicate, for Mrs. En–l—d was only a wife *pro tempore;* madam was thruft out of doors, and G—y kicked out without his tail. Poor G—y was afterwards fent to the fleet for debts contracted, which deprived him of indicting Dick for the affault. The reader will not wonder at Mrs. En–l—d's attachment to G—y, for he not only diverted her upon his violin, which he played on very well; but he had all the fim-plicity of manners that women like, and that forms fuch a contraft between a man of worldly knowledge, and the upftart *fcene-fhifter*.

near

near L——r-F—ds, and a greek alfo; the French greek would not pay, and Dick cut off the Frenchman's tail quite clofe. Poor little G—y Ma—n fhared the fame fate, though from another caufe.

The unrelenting perfeverance of Dick, aftonifhed other low greeks at firft, but it had this fatal confequence at laft, they made a bold pufh at all horfe-races, cock-fights, &c. fo true it is with low minds, " they firft look on, then pity, then em- " brace."

The fate of poor Rowles lives in the breaft of every feeling mind; but though it muft freeze the foul with horror, we relate it with all its ferious confequences, that thofe who were then infants, may now be on their guard, and never mix with fuch monfters.

Mr. Rowles was fond of play, as many men of unfullied honour are. Dick forced him to play, when Mr. R. was much in-toxicated; the confequence proved that Dick made a demand of 200 g——. Mr. R. ever denied lofing a guinea; and always afferted that he was too drunk to play: however,

however, nor laws divine, nor human, could weigh with this fiend. He followed him from place to place; and at laſt forced him to degrade human nature, by drawing a trigger * with him. Not content with attempting to rob him of 200 guineas, he took *aim*, and deprived Mr. R. of his life, and the town of Kingſton of a worthy and upright man.

Juſtice, though ſlow, is very ſure; and though this blood-thirſty ſavage took to immediate flight, we hope, and devoutly wiſh, this monſter will ſome day be brought to condign puniſhment.————While Ld. D—ry † lives he cannot come here, which
we

* Dick was known conſtantly to praſtice at firing at a mark, but his great luxury was ſhooting at a poor cat, and he would make a bet of ten or twenty, that he lodged a bullet in its head, or as he termed it, ſinge the whiſkers of poor puſs. We need not inform the philo-ſopher, nor the enlightened reader, that ſingeing the whiſkers is a *rank bull*; for bullets, though fatal, carry no degree of heat with them, of courſe, this ignoramus was wrong in his conceptions, as to the power of heat.

† This nobleman, well known for his politeneſs and humanity, as moſt of the real Iriſh gentlemen are, was
preſent

we have great reafon to lament; for though fled from juftice, he has been ever fince practifing his Greek fyftem in France; and, at

prefent at the unhappy duel, and gave his evidence with that elegance and precifion, that the coroner's inqueft pronounced murder againft R—h—d En–l—d, alias Captain En–l—d; and though officers of juftice were difpatched to every port in the kingdom, and hand-bills ftuck up at the corner of every ftreet through London and Weftminfter. yet Dick, having better luck than his crimes merited, got landed upon the coaft of France, where we fhould devoutly wifh Providence to continue him, were it not for the depredations that he is now committing on our Englifh nobility and gentry, who travel generally with their tutor to improve their mental faculties, and give them a knowledge of the world. We are forry to fay, and we fpeak with infinite regret (with very few exceptions) that they return without benefiting either head or heart, and generally *fans argent*, and what is ftill worfe, with a very impaired conftitution. Lord Chefterfield, whofe profound knowledge of the world ftrictly enjoined his heir never to enter that fink of fin and iniquity, called Italy; if he had juft faid as much of France, he would have added to his great portion of wifdom: for the beft that ever could be faid of the French nobility, to fpeak truly, is, that they are a groupe of frivolity and infincerity; practifing all the modern vices the nobles of this country fall into, excepting intemperance; for fobriety has a claim to univerfal

C approbation;

at this moment is in partnerſhip with the
chaſte Dian — Lady W——·y, of bathing
memory. At the various watering places
he was a terror to urbanity, and not content
with inſulting any gentleman he thought
proper, he often ſaid the moſt impertinent
things to ladies, who were deaf to his jar-
gon, and importuning them to dance a
cowtillion—for ſo he called it.

Here reaſon and humanity cries aloud :
What, were there no brother, father, or
that unfaſhionable thing—a *huſband*, to re-
ſent his impudence ?—No ; the gentlemen,
in every inſtance, conſidered him beneath
contempt.

At landing a dye, Dick ſhone unrivalled.
But his *diſpatches* * turned to his greateſt
emolument ; as he would often ſwear by
Jaſus ! there is nothing *aqual* to a few pigeons

approbation ; and this virtue alone is the only good
quality the Frenchmen are bleſſed with in an eminent
degree, and compenſates ſomewhat for other defeĉts.

* A cant phraſe for dice that have juſt ſo many ſpots,
that are not regularly marked, but are ſo numbered that
the thrower cannot poſſibly loſe.

with

with a pair of difpatches. The flip *—the bridge †—the brief ‡, &c. he was expert at; for nature had been prolific in giving him a hand the fize of a fhoulder of mutton— and of courfe a pack of cards could be very eafily concealed; and has been to the ruin of many unfufpecting generous minds.

If we may be allowed to leave this mifcreant a moment, we are happy to in-

* The flip is when the cards are cut. The party that deals, puts the fame cards again at top, and if he is an adept, as Dick was, he will defy the eyes of argus to deteĉt him; of courfe, having planted the cards prior to the cut, he is fure to win, and good play is of no ufe.

† The bridge is a bend of any particular card, fo that he may cut to it, and have it dealt to him when his adverfary deals.

‡ The brief is a card either wider or longer than any other card in the pack; they generally get fupplied with fuch cards from ——— ——— ———, a well known bankrupt card-maker; who, when in a ftate of intoxica- tion, has been often known to fay, that he muft go and touch the greeks in Pall-Mall for twenty or thirty if he pleafed, or he would blow them up, i. e. expofe them. The partnerfhip of greek houfes fet down this under the head of hufh money.

troduce

troduce a well-known fact, and muſt record
it to the praiſe of his Royal Highneſs the
Duke of Clarence *, for his invariable op-
poſition to play of any kind: we hope not
only the naval officers, but the army alſo
will profit by his wiſe and illuſtrious ex-

* We feel unutterable ſatisfaction, and we doubt not
but it will be an exultation of great comfort throughout
the kingdom *(greeks excepted)* to relate the following
anecdote.

Admiral Ba——g—n invited his Royal Highneſs,
with a number of naval officers to dine, they all met, of
courſe, as punctual to their time as they are obſervers
of their duty, the Prince excepted, who made an
elegant excuſe, though he only kept them five minutes.
The day paſt in the utmoſt harmony, and no play, or
even a hint of play took place. We are happy to
add, that this meeting is to take place the enſuing winter; and we hope for the honour, the felicity, and health
of his Majeſty's officers by ſea and land, that many
ſuch convivial meetings will be eſtabliſhed, which will
greatly facilitate to put that deteſtable vice of high-
gaming out of countenance, and make their wives,
their ſons, and daughters happy, in knowing what their
fathers ſo nobly fought and bled for, will be ſecured
againſt the invaſion of a cormorant black-leg, without
either head or heart, and dead to every human feeling,
excepting the vitious one of wiſhing to rob every family
in the kingdom.

ample.

ample. On this fcore his Royal Highnefs
has made a few enemies; but is there one
prudent mind in this kingdom, that will not
give him the warmeft tribute of applaufe?
and the name of Clarence be ever held in
the higheft reverence for courage, loyalty,
prudence, and humanity.

We would gladly clofe the dark catalogue
of fuch a mifcreant as Dick En–l—d, but
cannot. We therefore ferioufly hope and
fupplicate, that a law may pafs the next
feffions of parliament, to banifh any man
the realm who is known to live by play;
or what is commonly called a black-leg.

The ftory of poor Clutterbuck * is frefh
in the memory of every body. Dick, with
his

---

* Clutterbuck was a clerk in the bank of England,
and came from reputable parents: but we cannot help
lamenting that the moft important part of children's
education is not ferioufly attended to in this great city,
namely, Public Worfhip, and a profound and folemn
undeviating reverence for the Sabbath Day. Had he
but once known the invaluable bleffing of ferving his
Creator, and felt it as his firft and moft important duty
to keep the Sabbath holy, he would never have been
forfaken. The promifes of God are immutable, " his

" ways

his new partner Jack T———n, had so prac-
tised upon him that he not only lost his all,
but robbed the bank of an immense sum to
pay his debts of *honour*.

The late Capt. Tom Ro———h of greek
memory, had, unhappily for himself, a very
disagreeable breath; Dick, who had always
viewed the Captain as his rival with a jaun-
dice eye, said to him one night, at that *pious*
and *immaculate* house called Me—ly's, " By
Jasus, Captain, your breath stinks da-n—ly!"
" How can it be otherwise, replied the Captain, when I sit near you, who are a mass
, of pollution." Dick was dumb; for though
Ro———h was known to live by play, yet
he had a pleasantry and manners about him
that partly reconciled a man, if he even
lost a few pounds to him ; his company was

" ways are ways of pleasantness, and all her paths are
" peace."

It came out in evidence, that though this youth devi-
ated from the paths of virtue, he lost most of his money
at Richmond, to T———n and others, of a Sunday. We
hope to see the day, that when clerks in such public
trust are seen at any of those places of vice and folly,
that after a proof clearly made, they shall be held un-
worthy their office.

worth

worth it, as company now goes. But there
is fuch a thing as paying an over-price, and
we fhall be happy if our young readers will
profit by the hiftory of this hero.

At Newmarket a quarrel happened between a gentleman of black-leg fame and
Dick, about their *honefty ;* Dick accufing
him of always having loaded dice in his
pocket, for the purpofe of robbing the inexperienced generous youth. The black-leg,
in a manner peculiar to their order, replied,
" And if I have, d—n your eyes, I know you
have them alfo ; and what's more, bl—t
you, I will bet you fifty I know who makes
them for you." Dick called him a great
thief and liar, and here the matter ended.
But fuch a converfation muft convince every
mind of common underftanding, there is a
powerful, nay an awful reafon, why dice
fhould be entirely put a ftop to ; as nothing fhort of prohibition can have the
leaft effect.

The following well-known fact alone
fhould animate every member of both houfes
of parliament to exert their unwearied purfuits to obtain a law fo long and devoutly

wifhed

wifhed for by all ranks in fociety; but the peft of greeks.

The Hon. Mr. Da—r, who, a few years ago, fhot himfelf at Stacie's, told the fub-fequent melancholy tale, prior to his diffo-lution: That having often often played at tennis with Sir Wm. Dr——r, and other gentlemen of equal honour, for amufe-ment and exercife only; he, one day, at an unpropitious moment, not knowing his company, played tennis with Dick, who complimented Mr. Da—r on the ufe of his racket, that he could not encounter him again, unlefs he gave him odds, &c.

The experienced man of the world will readily credit Dick at fineffe; for though he loft a few guineas, he conld have won to a certainty. Such is the mutability of human nature that, Mr. Da—r, who we are warranted to affert, would not have walked round Ranelagh with Dick, or had him at his table for twenty thoufand pounds; yet he fell a victim to this infernal villain's deep-laid ftratagem.

Dick, with more of the banditti, fent to Paris for the beft tennis-player in the world.

The

The Frenchman was let into the fyſtem that he was often to loſe; but when he had the office * given him by Dick, he was then to win.

Dick was all this time nurſing the amiable, unfuſpicious, and ever-to-be-lamented Mr. Da––r; for while Dick was ſeemingly backing Mr. Da––r, for forty, fifty, and ſometimes an hundred guineas a ſet, Mr. Da––r was loſing three, four, and ſometimes five thouſand guineas in a day; and with ſuch blind avidity did he purſue this deſtructive game, that he found himſelf a loſer of near forty thouſand guineas :––at laſt (alas! too late) he found it prudent to reſiſt thoſe infernal dæmons, who after they had ſo plundered him, were conſtantly in Tilny-Street, requeſting payment, or part. It is ſaid, Mr. Da––r offered them poſt-obits––bonds––or, in ſhort, the beſt ſecurity he could then offer––his father, then L––d

_____

* A ſignal given as agreed on previous to their morning's play, either by a white or red handkerchief, or taking their hat of, and various other ſigns, as theſe raſcals ſuggeſted; not uſing the ſame ſign twice, leaſt they may be ſmoak'd.

D   Me––––n,

Me———n, now E—l of D———e, being alive : no ; they would have cafh :—Mr. Da—r could not find it ; but to his high fenfe of honour, be it told, he threw himfelf at his father's feet ; the worthy parent weighed the matter well, and fent his fteward from M———n-Abbey with power to pay every fhilling, though he knew his fon had been cheated of every guinea—when, oh! dreadful to relate, the venerable, the faithful fteward arrived a few hours too late, and had the heart-rending fight of his young and truly beloved mafter weltering in his gore, having fhot himfelf as we obferved before at Stacie's. There are other circumftances relative to this tragedy * ;
but

---

* Prior to Mr. Da—r's putting the piftol to his temple, he fent for five or fix wh—es, and a man, well known about the Garden, called Blind Burnett, a fidler; and while they were in the act of dancing and finging, he fent himfelf to that bourne from whom no traveller ever did return. We lament exceedingly, that, in the higher orders of fociety, where wifdom fhould go hand in hand with affection, that parents in general, without confulting the genius and inclinations of their children; a large fortune on the one fide, or a title on the other, are made the firft objects of their care.

In

but as they are more like infanity than the
act of a mind, greatly expanded by a
polifhed

In the prefent unhappy cafe before us, Mr. Da—r
married a daughter of General C—w—y's, a lady per-
feftly accomplifhed and truly virtuous; and though thefe
are prominent features in the eye of human difcernment,
yet fhe was too fond of bringing marble from its rude
ftate of nature, into a fine likenefs of our moft gracious
and ever-to-be-adored fovereign. Had there been no
male ftatuary in this country, for the high compenfation
of having in marble one of the beft fovereigns that ever
wielded a fceptre, we fhould have had lefs caufe to
lament that fhe thought more of chipping, and her
chifel, than fhe did of fecuring the affeftions of the
young, the gay, the generous, and the accomplifhed
Da—r, her hufhand.

Sam. Johnfon, of diftionary fame, and better authority
we need not quote, obferves, that ninety-nine men out
of one hundred would be good hufbands, provided the
women did their duty by them; and we beg to add, that
if gentlemen of the haut ton, inftead of permiting their
wives to turn night into day, and paying not the fmalleft
regard to the Sabbath, would aft with a moral and
religious firmnefs, things would be much better; and
we might cherifh a hope, that example may fucceed to
the certain benefit of millions, and the honour of
human nature. At prefent, nothing is more common
than to fee my lord and his lady, with a circle of friends,
on the Sabbath night *(Oh, fhame! where is thy blufh!)*
playing

polifhed education, and a fuavity of manners, rarely to be excelled in this or any
other country; we do not doubt but a
phrenzy of the mind had deprived him
of all his faculties, and caufed this never-
to-be-forgotten fatal cataftrophe.

We doubt not but his noble and honourable brothers will, in every point, emulate

playing cards in the drawing-room; while the butler,
the coachman, the footman, the cook, and the reft of
this *pious* family are amufing themfelves in the kitchen.
One fhould think that it does not require a very fapient
mind to find out the different numbers and names of
fifty-two cards; but a recent inftance is a proof to the
contrary. A certain duke had what is called a private
party on a Sunday night to play; the fervants would
have been *happy* in paffing the evening in the fame way,
but they faid, *that as how, if fo be they had kings, and
queens, and knaves dealt them,* they did not know a queen
from a knave. One of the knights of the fhoulder knot,
thought of an expedient to pafs the evening in dancing,
and had the decenfy, as it was the Sabbath-Day, to
dance without a fiddle—and though a majority of the
motley crew vowed and *purtefled* that the Duke of
Gl—cef—r had mufic every Sunday, and that they had
as good a right to a fiddle as the duke had. To expect
thefe fellows, who are a thoufand times better fed than
taught, to know the difference betwixt facred mufic and
a country dance, would be very unreafonable.

Mr.

Mr. Da—r's exalted chara&er, and, by his example, avoid monſters, that high-waymen and ſtreet robbers are innocence itſelf to.

As our hero had given up his attention to billiard-tables, unlefs a flat * was known to be fond of the game, his time was di-vided in the following manner, for the *public good.*

Tennis in the morning ; or riding out to find a pigeon. Dining at ſeven, for he aped the great world in every thing but their virtues and their graces. The dinner over, a little play for trifles would be propoſed, by a friend that always dropt in by ACCIDENT ; and ſome *how* or *other* Dick was ſo *generous*, Jack M—d—y would b—ſt his e—s that Capt. En-l—d always paid the reckoning for the whole company. The fa& was, the company loſt all their money.

---

* A cant phraſe for a fool, or one that does not know the game he is playing at. Though a man may be as wiſe as Solomon, and even play the game well, there is no guarding againſt a combination of thieves any other way, than to avoid them altogether.

An

An ill-fated hour, the Hon. Lieutenant Rochford, nephew to the Earl of Bel––d––re, had the misfortune to lofe all his cafh at a public hazard table. Dick, knowing his man, politely offered him any cafh he wanted, though Dick was an entire ftranger to him. Few young men of fafhion would have hefituted a moment, but Lieutenant Rochford did; at length he accepted his *polite* offer.

Rochford, had what is called a run of luck, and repaid our hero before he quitted the table. But fuch is the fallability of young minds, that though Rochford was counfelled by Col. L––––s to guard himfelf againft Dick, yet he actually (woman like) often frequented his houfe, and the more he was advifed not to affociate with him, the greater his propenfity. At laft, though Rochford was known to be a flat by the greeks; the world at large, or at leaft the greateft part confidered him a greek alfo; fo true it is that a good name is often got without merit, and oftener loft without deferving. For Rochford was what all real Irifh gentlemen are, generous, polite, en-
gaging,

gaging, and an inexhauſtible fund of good
humour, that conſtantly kept the table in a
roar: his perſonal accompliſhments kept
pace with his mental faculties; and unleſs
it was to keep an unlettered greek in order,
an ungentleman-like word never dropped
from his tongue. We ſhall now ſee the ſad,
ſad, conſequence of young men of birth and
education mixing with ſuch outcaſts of ſo-
ciety. Rochford was then encamped at
Warley-Common, and having been obſerv-
ed by a cenſorious brother officer to ſpeak
to Dick at the play, and other places of
public reſort, they of a ſudden grew very
cool upon him.

Rochford ſpiritidly aſked an explanation.
One of his brother officers informed him
that he was reported to keep company
with Dick En–l—d, and other black-legs
(for the word greek was not then known)
and of courſe they, as gentlemen of honour,
could not ſit with him.

This brought on a ſerious altercation, a
challenge, in a very polite way took place.
Poor Rochford ſet off from the camp to
adjuſt his affairs in London, and to pay his
reſpeets

refpects to a few real friends, and then
returned to meet his antagonift. We are
forry to fay, that Rochford received a ball
in his groin, which, in a few hours deprived
him of his life; leaving an amiable wife
and a young family, totally unprovided
for.

May we not exclaim with Addifon, " Is
there not fome thunder in the ftores of
heaven red with uncommon wrath, to blaft
the villain who owes his exiftence to fuch
nefarious practices."——No, Dick does not
think fo; or furely he would have taken
fome method to get an honeft livelihood—
fhifting a fcene, or blacking a fhoe, would
be paradife to it! for even Dick muft have
moments of remorfe, that no good man can
envy.

Though we do not charge our hero with
the murder of poor Rochford, yet we are
juftified in obferving, that if gaming had
been fuppreffed, as it ought for more than
twenty years back, Rochford, and many
other worthy characters, in all human pro-
bability, would have been now living, a
comfort

comfort to their family, and an ornament to fociety.

Mr. Ro—rd, a gentleman of more zeal than prudence, meeting Dick at Tatterfall's, foon after took him afide, and expoftulated with him thus.

" Really Mr. En–l—d, the death of poor Rochford muft be fet down to your account, for had you contented yourfelf with ftaying in Smock-Alley theatre, my poor coufin would have been, moft likely, now alive ; and I hope you will cut * the turf, dice, &c." " Blood and wounds, fir," replied Dick, " it was my *intereft* to let him live you know, and, by Jafus, I would have given fifty guineas to have prevented the *jewel*."

Our hero now had learned to write, and we are glad, as yet, no bad or fatal confequence has tranfpired from fo important an addition to his *larning*, for fo he calls it ; but though he could ufe his pen, he wanted rather more practice at reading, to make it of any ufe to him.

* A phrafe for leaving off, but generally underftood when you leave off a winner.

E   Having

Having a draft on Gofling the banker, for fifty guineas, he ordered the coachman to drive to Mr. Go–fling's, the great big banker in *Flate*-Street. Away drove poor cochée, and after driving up and down Fleet-Street for two hours, and no Go–fling to be found, Dick returned to St. Alban's-Street, and wrote Major C—— the following note.

" Mr. Major,

" By Chrift I *tuke* ye for a *gentelmen*, but
" by the living G–d, *bif yu* dont tack hup
" that bl—t–d piece of thick paper *whech*
" yu did give me, by the x of St. Patrick,
" I will dock you clofer then I did the
" French w——h-maker. Some *gentlemen*
" would have *hexpos'd* you by *fhowen* the
" name of Go–fling, when, by Jafus, there
" is no fuch name at all, *at all*; pay the
" fifty, or take your fate.

" Your *ingird* friend,

" R——d E——d."

On receipt of this *elegant* epiftle, the Major fent the following anfwer.

" Major

" Major C—— prefents his compliments
" to Capt. En–l—d, affures him that after
" infinite pains in decyphering his letter,
" Major C—— conceives Capt. En–l—d
" to be under fome miftake, Gofling the
" bankers, are too well known in Fleet-
" Street not to be found, and Major C——
" has too high a fenfe of honour, however
" he might have *loft* his fifty to Capt.
" En–l—d, not to pay it."

Dick fhewed the letter to Jack M——y
who could read. " Why bl—t you, you
Irifh thief," " fays Jack, " you are a fine
humbug, not to know a Gofling from Gofling. I'll give you a good hedge, there
is forty-eight guineas for your draft." Dick
took it, thinking that poor Jack was finely
taken in.

Jack, though lame, hobbled to Fleet-
Street, and immediately received the cafh
for Major C——'s draft, to the no fmall
diverfion of the *worthy* company of Round-
Court notoriety.

Mr. Blo—b—g, of ——, Yorkfhire, ufed
to tell the following ftory. Being at York
in the race-week, he after fupper propofed
to

to his brother-in-law I—c May—rd, to put
ten pound to his, and they would go to hell *
and fport it. Mr. May—rd, with his ufual
good humour, replied, " It was an odd
fancy, but he would make the bank twenty."
Away they fallied out, inquiring where
hell was kept this year. A fharp boy (for
there are no flats in York) anfwered them,
it is kept at the *clerks* of the *minfter,* in
Minfter-Yard, next to the church.

* Hell, fo called, and indeed very properly, is a
receptacle for the vileft crew that ever difgraced humanity. The highwayman, the fharper, the houfebreaker,
the bully, advertifing money lender, and pimp, generally form the motley groupe; though now and then
gentlemen of real honour affift their midnight orgies, by
way of fpeculation, or to *feavoir le monde,* and fome-
times, or they would have no trade, a few fimple phi-
lofophers in the neighbouring towns, and the fons of
our wealthy cits; for, to the honour of their fathers,
they knew much better than even to affociate with them.
We conjure our readers and worthy citizens to believe,
that, if they would only refrain from vifiting fuch
places, it would as effectually put a ftop to gaming, as
the moft powerful act of parliament ever paffed in our
fenate could devife; for they would not prey upon one
another—it would be diamond cut diamond according
to their text.

Our

Our two truly great and good characters, after being examined by the door-keeper, got admitted into this *honourable* and *pious* house ; here they found about thirteen black-legs, all of the lower order, Capt. En-l—d at the head. They had been playing, the Captain said, for some hours (fudge); they, strictly speaking, had not made a bet in *arnest*, as they call it. Though neither B——g or M—n—d had ever spoke to Dick, yet he began his old cant, that by *Jasus*, he had such a run of bad luck, that he must sell his horse, and go to the big city in the basket of the York fly. But make up ten guineas among you, said Dick, and break me at once. Mr. Bl—rg put down ten guineas, not with gold, but a *good luckin* note, as Dick called it; and Dick threw, called 7 is the mayne, if 7 or 11 is thrown next, the *caster* wins; but Dick made a blunder, and threw 12. The truth was, Dick had *landed* at 6, and the die he threw out of the box did not answer to his hopes ; it should have been a 5 to have made 11 ; and though 5 squares out of the 6 were dotted with 5 spots each, yet

yet our hero had the mifery of lofing his
bet; for 12 thrown after 7, makes the
cafter the lofer of the *main*. Without
being too fuperftitious, one might think
fate has now and then a hand in ftopping
the career of thefe vultures.

A fimple philofpher would have thought,
that having loft his bet, Mr. Bl—g would
have been paid: no, Dick, with matchlefs
effrontry, fwore he called 6 inftead of 7 for
the main; as in that cafe he would have
won; but Mr. May—rd, who was perfectly
fober, and whofe nice honour no man ever
doubted, told Dick, Mr. B——g had won,
and that he (Dick) called 7. Our hero
had another fubterfuge. " Mr. B——g,
replied Dick, " *if Jo be as how* you will
infift upon faying you have won, we muft
abide the majority." Mr. B——g, Mr.
May—rd, and another gentleman, were
the only three men of real honour; of
courfe, when it was put round, as they call
it, there appeared thirteen *honeft gemen* for
Dick, and two for Bl—g; he according to
the laws of hazard, could not vote. However, Mr. Bl—g thought it hard he fhould
be

be thus robbed; he attempted to take up
his ten guinea note, but Dick put his *little*
hand to a very large candleſtick, and ſwore
by Jaſus, he would *clave* his ſcull if he
touched his property. The two gentlemen
interfered, and left this groupe of *worthies*
to divide the ſpoil, for they were all part-
ners, and would have ſworn (dreadful even
to think) any thing Dick ordered them
to ſwear.

Mr. Scr——re, of the Weſt-Riding of
Yorkſhire, who had juſt finiſhed his ſtudies
at Cambridge, viſited his aunts on the ſpot
that gave him birth; unhappily for this
accompliſhed, though very credulous gentleman, our hero Dick ſeduced him to
play at Doncaſter races; an ignoramus
would think that Dick won: no, no, Dick
knew better, he let our young cantab win
a few guineas; they ſupped and parted.
Dick found (for he had always good intel-
ligence) Mr. Scr——re would be, when of
age, in poſſeſſion of about twelve hundred
pounds a year—of courſe a fine pigeon;
Dick ſhewed him every mark of *civility*,
and was *ſo kind* even to offer him his beſt

horſe

horfe to ride to the races, and alfo to let him go five or ten guineas with him upon a race: Dick was very *lucky*, for every day after the races were over, Dick paid Mr. Scr——re five or ten guineas per day as his proportion of winning; this fo pleafed our young ftudent, that he invited him to his feat to pafs a week or a fortnight: our hero knew better, he would have been *blown* upon as the greeks phrafe it; he had other purfuits; inviting in return Mr. Scr——re to his houfe, affuring him that he lived upon a fcale of œconomy, that he *contented* himfelf upon foup, fifh, and a bit of roaft or boiled for the *firft courfe*, and for the *fecond* he had a b——h cook that dreft his game very well and made an excellent pudding. If you can content yourfelf with that, continued our hero, I generally find a bottle of claret for a country friend, or a bowl of *rack* punch, and this, faid Dick, is *my way of living*. We invite the fympathifing heart, the foother of forrow and misfortune, ready to pity an inexperienced mind, whether from Cambridge or Oxford, and make every allowance for our youth

thus

thus entrapped. We would not begrudge
them to pay fmart money, if they would
ftop there; but the misfortune is, lured by
the hope of gain, and a defire to get into
a round of diffipation, they generally facri-
fice their health and the beft part of their
fortune. Mr. Scr——re wanting a few
months of age, and having no friend to
advife him but two maiden aunts, he vifited
the capital, of courfe left his card with
Capt. En-l—d; the Captain returned his
vifit, fent him an invitation to take a family
dinner next day at fix; Mr. Scr——re accepted the invitation, and found a *hopeful*
party, confifting of Capt. De Ch——u, a
well-known adept, and Dick's *ufeful* man,
Mrs. En-l—d, and two w——s; the latter
paffed for widows of Irifh gentlemen, with
immenfe jointures. Nothing very brilliant
paffed at dinner; the ladies fung, and Dick
entertained the company with his prowefs
in Ireland, having called out five men and
killed four of them,—that *jewelling* was
the fineft thing in the world, and that he
kept *jontlemen* always in order; Captain
De Ch——u was not behind hand, for he

averred, that though he loved peace and
good order, his body was all over fcars,
having fought thirty-fix duels and killed
twenty-eight. The ladies applauded their
valour, and obferved, *that as if fo be as how
gemmen* would be *wexatious*, they were ferved
very right. A bumper toaft was propofed
by our hoft; without conveying any thing
indelicate to our readers, we will leave
them to guefs what it was, though of late
years this has been a prevailing cuftom.
We hope, for the honour and happinefs of
the liberal and refined, that fuch toafts will
be entirely abandoned: but now the fatal
tragedy begins. Play was propofed, and
as it had been pre-determined by Dick, and
his other *friends*, to difh * the cantab over
as foon as they could, the difpatches were
put down on the table; the rack punch
pufhed about, made very *weak*†, and in
about

---

* Difh'd is a phrafe in great ufe with the *family* lads,
and means that the pigeon has loft all his money, his
fecurity of every kind, his horfes, and every valuable.

† So *cenforious* and naughty are the world grown, that
they do not hefitate to fay that our *noble* Capt. En–l—d
puts

about two hours the poor cantab loſt all his money, the contents of his pocket-book, and found himſelf in debt twelve hundred guineas. The cantab expreſſed his ſurpriſe at ſuch a run of ill luck ; they conſoled him, that after to-morrow's ride they would eat a bit of dinner at ſome tavern (though there were only two * in town would admit

the

puts a ſort of a kind of a drug, to be had of at every chemiſt's in town (though the *greeks* have a chemiſt of their own) when his friends won't drink freely. But men of diſcernment cannot believe that ſo *noble* an hoſt as Dick would do any thing half ſo *bad :*—this is really too cruel; and we hope none but thoſe, whoſe intereſt it is, will credit it.

* There are but two houſes that will admit greeks in parties; individually they ſcour the town; they have their runners in pay like Swiſs ſoldiers; and not a coffee-houſe from Mile-End to Tatterſall's, but they are upon the look-out. We cannot help lamenting that our privy-council would iſſue a proclamation to ſend thoſe *induſ-tirous,* brave, *upright, learned,* and *wiſe* men to explore the northern climes of America, or lend them to our good friend and ally the Empreſs of R——a.

We will not deſcribe the two houſes that admit this diabolical crew of greeks : but, if the public, who are always curious, will inquire of the neighbours in C——y-Street, near C——y-Market, for that frequented by the

lower

the greeks) and give him his revenge. The
ſtudent borrowed a guinea to pay his chair,
and

lower order of *greeks* and *affidavit men* :—its the head of
Shakeſpeare to a Moorfields ballad, but the neighbours
will kindly tell the inquirer.

The other *worthy* is ſo well known by the *rude* appel-
lation of Black J—k, that there is not a link or ſhoe boy
that would not point to the B——d A—s. The turf
will meet with an irreparable loſs, ſhould this gent——n
die a *natural* death, as *he bl-——d his eyes and l——hs
tha: he has loſt his whole fortune on theſe* " *here four legged
beaſteſſes.*"

With what pleaſure do we retouch the memory of thoſe
who from hurry or any other cauſe, might have forgot
the conduct of Williams, who keeps a tavern and coffee-
houſe in Bow-Street, and who is alſo (much to his
credit) a comedian.

Laſt winter, Williams, with his uſual prudence, ſhut
his ſtreet door at a proper hour. At about twelve, or
between twelve and one, he heard a violent knocking
at his door ; when aſking who was there ? he was an-
ſwered with an oath—two or three gentlemen : thinking
them ſo, Williams opened the door, and to his unutterable ſurpriſe, he found the gentlemen to be Jack
T——g—n, Capt. A——, and a flat.

Williams knowing the two *worthies,* ſaid, " I have
no room for ſuch gentlemen as you ; my houſe is not
for gamblers ; you may go where you pleaſe, but you
ſhan't come here." The two worthies talked of their
conſequence :

and went to his hotel. The thoughts of lofing fuch a fum, Mr. Scr——re has often

confequence: they afked him, "if he knew who they were;" "Yes, replied the honeſt and worthy fon of Thefpis, "I do know *you,* and therefore won't let you in;" a fcuffle enfued, and what is very ſtrange, thefe *worthies* indiĉed poor honeſt Williams for an aſſault: the trial came on in the Common-Pleas, and the aſſault was proved, by Williams owning he took them by the coat or collar, and puſhed them off the ſtep of his houfe.

Lord Loughborough, in his fumming up, told the jury, that the aſſault had been proved, but under fuch circumſtances that he hoped, nay, he did not doubt, but they would give fuch damages as would deter men of fuch defcription and notoriety, ever ſhewing themfelves as plaintiffs in that or any other court of judicature.

THE JURY,

TO THEIR IMMORTAL HONOUR,

WITHOUT

ONE MOMENT'S HESITATION,

PRONOUNCED

DAMAGES FOR THE PLAINTIFFS

ONE HALFPENNY!

Bravo! criedReafon; LOUGHBOROUGH, the JURY, and WILLIAMS for Ever!

N. B. This aĉtion is on record, A. D. 1792.

declared,

declared, deprived him of any thing like
fleep that night. They met and dined the
next day, and fortune was fuch a *jilt*—made
the twelve hundred eighteen hundred more,
and as a little ready was wanted, and he an
entire ftranger in town (having loft both
father and mother) they *generoufly* lent him
twenty guineas for his purfe, propofing to
the ftudent to pay them in three notes of
one thoufand guineas each, two days after
he became of age.

This child of fimplicity now began to
think ferioufly, and upon afking the mafter
of the M—t coffee-houfe (for the mafter
knew Scr——re's father) he in the moft un-
referved manner told him what all the
gentlemen faid of them, namely, that they
were notorious black-legs, and that not one
man of honour in the kingdom would fit
down with them.

Our ftudent had given the notes, and
money had been advanced upon them by
an *honeft* lawyer; for though the act prevents
a man from being forced to pay more than
ten pounds loft at one fitting, yet, when
they are indorfed from one to another, and
good

good proof cannot be produced, the poor flat not only gives his notes, but through the chicane of the petty-fogger, and a few *affidavits*, he is often obliged to pay.

Mr. Scr——re, by this time had made himfelf known to fome of his neighbours, and cut with his two *worthy* and *friendly* *acquaintance*.

The late and much beloved Sir Charles Tu—er, ufed to obferve to Mr. Scr——re, that it was the beft three thoufand guineas he ever parted with, for he never played fince.

We are forry to produce another inftance of the weaknefs of mankind. Mr. Da—n, of very confiderable landed property, in and near Newcaftle upon Tyne, determined to vifit the watering places, and to finifh his tour with paffing a week or ten days at Scarborough. Our hero Dick, with one of his brigade, obferving a chaife drive through the town, difpatched a courier to inquire the gentleman's name, where he came from, and what ftay he would make, &c. The courier returned with every re-quifite information, and the next thing was

how

how to get at Da—n before he got to the
affembly-rooms.

Dick's inventive faculties were never idle,
he waited till he came out of the inn, and
modeftly fell into chat with him. After fome
converfation, Dick finding him a *dove*, he
offered Mr. Da—n his bed for that night,
for that he (Dick) could fleep at the coffee-
houfe; dryly obferving, " Perhaps my ap-
partment may do for both : for *if fo be* you
are an early *goer* to bed, and rife to bathe,
why in that cafe it will do for both; for I
never go to bed till feven at the *foonefl* in
the morning. Mr. Da—n thanked him for
his polite offer, but declined the honour of
his invitation.

The affembly over, the company formed
themfelves into parties as ufual, and happy
would it have been for Mr. Da—n if he
had made one among them ; but though a
man of an ancient and very honourable
family, he found but one perfon he knew,
and they were not on good terms.

This proved lucky for Dick and his
brigade (all Irifh); they ordered a fupper
at the coffee-houfe (for Donner would not

permit

permit any plunder, as he very properly called it, in his houfe). The glafs went merrily round, and about three in the morning Mr. Da—n was completely drunk. They had tried every effort to make him play, but in vain—of courfe, he muft fome how pay the reckoning. The brigade, to fave appearances, left any *improper* queftions were afked the waiter, played on for five or fix minutes longer, and then they each marked a card thus :—Da—n owes me two hundred guineas :—Da—n owes me one hundred and ninety-five guineas :—Da—n owes me fifty guines. Dick being the *great* man, marked his card thus :—I owe Da—n thirty guineas :——fo that deducting this fc—n—l's thirty guineas from the other fums, they made a tolerable night of it. The waiter, for they are *all* good fellows, touch'd five guineas for his care and atten- tion, the brigade parted, and poor Da—n. The next morning, or noon rather, for it was one o'clock, Dick accofted Mr. Da—n upon the cliff, " Well fir, how do you do after your night's regale? upon my con- fcience we were all very merry". " Yes",

G replied

replied the dove, " we were indeed, fir, and
I hope I did nothing to offend; for what
with the fatigue of travelling all day, and
your *good* company, Bacchus prevailed too
powerfully, and banifhed the little reafon
that I have entirely from me; but as I am
happy to hear no gentleman was offended,
all is very well."

Dick prefented him with a thirty guinea
banker's note, payable to R——d En–l—d,
Efq. faying, "I loft this *here* thirty to you laft
night, put it in your pocket, and I hope *we*
fhall have better luck another time." Da—n
ftared, and pofitively denied having played
for a fhilling; but Dick affured him upon
his honour that he had, obferving that he
had paid thoufands to gentlemen when in
liquor, that knew nothing at all of the
matter till he fhewed them his account.
Mr. Da—n fell into the trap fo infernally
laid for him, and being a novice, put the
thirty guineas into his pocket, thinking
Dick the moft upright man he ever met
with: when ftrange to relate, the *brigade*,
(all captains) came to the rooms in the evening full of complaifance, and each with a
brogue,

brogue, as ſtrong upon them as an Iriſh chairman, declared by the immaculate G–d how glad they were to ſee him well after ſuch a debauch.

George Bre—ton, the ſecond in command, ſhewed him his card : " My dear ſir I touch'd you for two hundred laſt night, and I'd thank you to give it me, for tomorrow I leave the North, and your two hundred will juſt take me to Dublin." This is what the greeks call a pretty commence; Mr. Da—n thunderſtruck with the demand, averred upon his honour, that he never played with him, and indeed he did not know of his playing at all, but that Captain En–l—d, very much to his credit, had paid him thirty guineas, though he did not remember a ſingle circumſtance of a card or dice being in the room. George replied with great warmth, " Sir, this is the firſt time my *honour* was ever doubted ; the *gentlemen* will all tell you, and ſo will the *waiter*, that I won two hundred guineas of you, though I cut a great loſer by the night's play." Mr. Da—n with his uſual moderation ſaid, " Sir, I ſhall have the pleaſure pleafure to fee you at the coffee-houfe to-morrow morning, and I make no doubt but matters will be amicably fettled.

The morning proved a propitious one for Mr. Da—n, for the preceding evening arrived about eight or nine of his friends and neighbours, perfons of great worth: Mr. Da—n opened his mind to them, they knew the world well; and after ten minutes converfation, and one of the gentlemen crofs-examining the *honeſt* waiter, the waiter prevaricated fo much, that to get rid of the bufinefs, and having received a promife of five guineas more if he told the truth, he affured the friend of Mr. Da—n that he did not know that Mr. Da—n played at all, or if he did, it could not be for five minutes altogether, as they were conftantly ringing and making *punch* in their *own* way.

Such complicated villany we feldom hear of.——The gentlemen then advifed Da—n not to pay a fhilling; but he propofed to them that he would fend Dick the thirty guinea banker's draft back to him, and add twenty more to pay the fupper, which was approved of by all prefent.

Mr.

Mr. Da—n wrote as follows :

" SIR,

" I ENCLOSE you your thirty guinea
" note, alfo twenty guineas more to pay
" the fupper that you invited me to on
" Wednefday night : I am forry to add that
" neither you nor either of your three
" friends have any claim to the rank of
" gentlemen, and of courfe I fhall treat
" you as fuch.   To Mr. George Bre—ton,
" nor either of the other *officers* (for they all
" wore very large cockades) will I ever
" fpeak to or pay a fhilling.

" I truft my conduct through life has
" been uniformly that of a man of ftrict
" probity, and nothing that you can fay
" will wound my honour or make me
" uneafy.   You are *well known* here by
" upwards of four hundred gentlemen, and
" though they are all ftrangers to me,
" except nine or ten, if one gentleman of
" refpectability will fay I ought to pay, I
" will pay with pleafure ; but I am con-
" vinced no fuch gentleman is to be
" found."

This

This letter was thunder to Dick, and acted like electric fire to the brigade.

George Br——n fwore he would have his liver broiling on the coals : the two junior brigades, who acted as fubordinate officers were dumb : at laft George Br——n began. " You fee Dick this is your bl—ed character that has da—d all ; as to me, what can they fay of me ? I, by Jafus, that am defcended from all the kings of Ireland ! and as to his being cheated, how can he prove that ?"—then turning to the two forlorn and miferable brigades, that had doubtlefs counted upon their cafh being paid, " You had better get out of town to night, as you are blown upon ; I cant fpeak to you, nor would it be prudent." But Dick fwore by Jafus, no :—they fhould each fend Da—n a challenge. This was over-ruled, as only one of the brigade could write : however, at laft it was re-folved, that K——n fhould write for the two ; and after much debate, the following curious epiftle was fent to Mr. Da—n.

" S I R,

" S I R,

" I AM *towld* by Capt. En-l—d, who *his*
" a man of *onner*, *that as how you wont*
" pay me one *honderd* and ninety *hod* gui-
" neas ; now by the great G-d of thunder
" and ftorms, if you do not fend it me in
" three fkips of a flea, after you have *red*
" my letter, de—l burn me but I will
" make a faggot of you, and put your
" a—e behind the fire. I care not what
" they fay about me a l—fe, for by Jafus,
" I am an Irifhman; and what's more, a
" volunteer; and what's more then all, I
" wont be *bother'd* by any *feler* in this
" here place. My dear little friend *to*,
" muft have his fifty, or you had better
" *ate* your fhoes; for by Jafus we have
" kill'd dozens in *duils*, and we will never
" flinch. But do what is right, and we are
" friends.

" We arĕ both your *obadent* fervants,

" R. K——n.

" The mark of C. O'G——n.

" *P. S.* Our ftay wont be ten *minits* for
" your *hanfer.*"

This

This curious epiftle being finifhed, George Br——n caft his indignant eye over it, and looking at the writer with a fneer— " Arrah, where did you go to fchool; by Mars, I fwear I never faw fuch a fpecimen before." Dick obferved, " What was *larning?* or what is fpelling? or what is Greek or *Welch*, or any of the modern dead or alive goffip? Dont you fee how Father Oburn lives upon butter-milk and tatys, and he *fpakes* forty or fifty *tongues*; plays the fiddle at wakes; fells twine, *bacco*, and cow-heels: and do you think that if there was any good in *larning*, Father Oburn would do that?" George fmiled with in-effable contempt—but the young brigade, who had juft made his *mark*, fwore by the Pope's bull, Capt. En–l—d was right; and added, " do you think me fuch a flat? no, no, my honey, no writing for me, 'tis dan-gerous; I might have been tempted to forge you know, and that's a *farvice* of danger." Dick, to fave appearance, went out of Scarborough the next morning by day-break, and took up two of his brigade a few miles on the York road.

The

The only one now remaining of the Irifh brigade was George Br––––n, and he finding neither threats nor artifice would provoke Mr. Da––n, in three mornings after left Scarborough (vowing vengeance on Mr. Da––n and all the bl–t–ed crew) to the great joy of all the ladies, and the heart-felt comfort of every good member of fociety. To do George Br––––n juftice, though he was not overburthened with a great ftore of literature, yet he knew more about reading and fpelling, and was very expert at *accompts*.

K––––n, though a fubaltern brigade, not lefs famed for his *prowefs*;––he made an effort of genius one night at the opera, and *fancied* a very fine gold enamelled box would be an addition to his toilet ;––took it *quietly* out of C. O––––'s pocket, and putting it into his own, was making *flow* ftrides through the lobby : the gentleman, miffing his box, purfued and took him.

Merciful as our juries are, in making allowances for youth, neceffity, or feduction ; they knew him an old and daring offender, and recommended their country

H   to

to pay his expences, and give him a paſſage to Botany-Bay.

We now take our leave of the *worthy* Dick; and as to his *amiable* connexions, we think a better leſſon need not be given the young mind, than briefly to ſtate the exit of thoſe robbers of all that's dear to ſo-ciety.

C. O'Geo—n made too *free* with a gen-tleman on Finchly-Common, and after a very impartial trial, was found guilty, and ſuffered death. Our laws, juſtly famed for their excellence, is always inclined to mercy; but in ſome caſes mercy would be cruelty. It is well known that the Old-Bailey juries are (very much to their honour) in general the moſt merciful men in the world; nor can the annals of this country produce a ſingle inſtance, wheie the courts of law had more able—more ſapient—and truly virtuous characters, than the preſent twelve judges.

George Br——n had his head cut off at one ſtroke, by a real officer of the army, then quartered in Dublin: George, who

had

had long been the terror of Daly's*, in-
fulted this much beloved fon of Mars in
the public coffee-room; and thinking to
bully the officer by menacing him, the
officer refented it, and George *meant* to
have fought a duel with *piftols†*; but the
officer poffeffing that true courage that a
Briton is famed for throughout the world,
infifted upon his being no better than a
vile *affaffin;* that it was well known · he
daily practifed *firing* at a mark, and of
courfe he would give him (George) the
choice of either fmall fword, or a cut and
thruft, as it is very properly called; George
accepted of the latter. The officer with
that firmnefs which invariably attends a
good caufe, made a parry at George's
firft blow, and (to the joy of all Dublin) in

* A club formerly of the firft nobility and gentry in
Dublin; but now a fubfcription houfe by ballot for play.

† George Br——n grew at laft fo callous that he ufed
to exult that he hoped to be thundered into a *nut-fhell* if
he could not take off a man's eye-brow, or hit his
button-hole. The truth is, George Br——n had a very
fteady hand, and what he called piftols, that would go off
with the touch of a feather.

the

the fecond parry, with a back ſtroke *ſever'd*
George Br——n's head from his body*.

We ſhall not detain our worthy readers
with many comments on this rencounter,
but juſt obſerve with Addiſon, " That
though the ways of heaven are dark, intri-
cate, puzzled, in error, and perplexed in
mazes ; nor can we, or is it fitting we ſhould,
know where the regular confuſion ends;"
it is enough to know, that heaven, though
ſlow, is juſt in ſaying to thoſe monſters,
" Hither ſhall you go and no further, and
here ſhall your vices end."

We cannot help obſerving, that the
Engliſh who have not travelled, too haſtily

---

* The officer ſurrendered at the next aſſize, and the

J   U   R   Y,

TO THEIR UNSPEAKABLE HONOUR,

RETURNED A VERDICT

N O T   G U I L T Y;

TO THE ENTIRE SATISFACTION

OF A VERY

CROWDED AND BRILLIANT COURT.

draw

draw conclufions (from a few fcore of thofe mifcreants coming here, wearing cockades, and looking terrible at every public place); to the traveller and philofopher it is well known the real gentlemen of Ireland are equal in learning, hofpitality, honour, and truth, to any nation round the globe, and pay the moft undeviating and kind attention to the Englifh, whether nobility, gentry, or man of commerce, that is known to deferve their efteem.

F   I   N   I   S.